W9-BZR-656

DATE DUE

ENCYCLOPAEDIA BRITANNICA
EDUCATIONAL CORPORATION
310 S. Michigan Avenue • Chicago, Illinois 60604

85354

My

Sound Box

by Jane Belk Moncure
illustrated by Linda Sommers

THE CHILD'S WORLD

MANKATO, MN 56001

Library of Congress Cataloging in Publication Data

Moncure, Jane Belk.
  My s sound box.

  (Sound box books)
  SUMMARY: A little boy fills his sound box with many
words that begin with the letter "s".
  [1. Alphabet books] I. Sommers, Linda. II. Title.
III. Series.
PZ7.M739Mys   [E]   77-8970
ISBN 0-913778-95-8 -1991 Edition

My "s" Sound Box

(The "sh" sound is included in this book along with blends.)

Little  had a

"I will find things that begin with my "s" sound," he said.

"I will put them into my sound  box."

 Little **S** took off his shoes,

his socks,

his   sweater,

and his shirt.

Did he put the shoes, socks, sweater, and shirt into his box? He did!

Little  put on his  swimsuit

and his sandals

and went
for a walk
on the
sand.

9

He found a shovel and a sand pail.

He made a sand castle.

Then he put the
shovel and the sand pail
and the sand castle into his box.

Little S went for a swim in the sea.

He saw a seal

swimming in the sea.

He saw six seals on the sand.
Did he put seven seals into his box?

He did!

Little found sea shells all over the sand.

He also found a  starfish.

Did he put the sea shells and
the starfish into his box?

He did!

Then he saw a 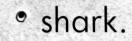 shark.

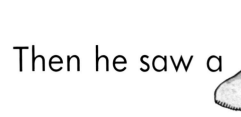

It was a small shark. So Little

slipped it into a 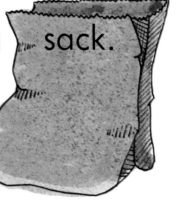 sack.

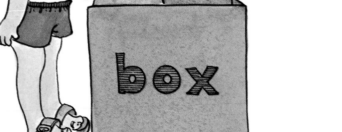

He put the sack
into the box.

Then Little  saw a sea snake.

It was a small sea snake,
so he slipped it
into the sack.

He put the sack back into the box.

Later, Little  met a sailor.

The sailor gave him

a  sailor hat.

"Let's play," said the sailor.

They played on the see-saw.

They slid
down the

slide.

Then they swang in the swings.

Suddenly, there was a big noisy sound!

The sound was coming from the box. "What is in the box?" asked the sailor.

"Things that begin with my "s" sound!" said Little S.

"I sail on things that begin with your sound," said the sailor. "I sail on a

ship.

And I sail on a

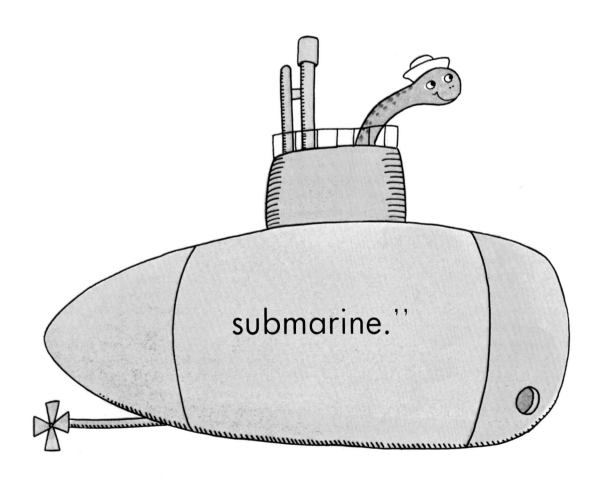

submarine."

The sailor helped Little  S bring his box into the submarine.

Little S took his

things out
of his box.

slide

sailor

swing

shoe

seven seals

shovel

sandals

sand pail

sand castle

starfish

And the sailor drew pictures of the ship, swing, slide, and see-saw.

ship

sea shells

swimsuit

sweater

shirt

shark

sea snake

sailor hat

sack

socks

see-saw

27

Can you read these words with Little S ?

stick

sunflower

snail

soap

star

sink

salad

seed

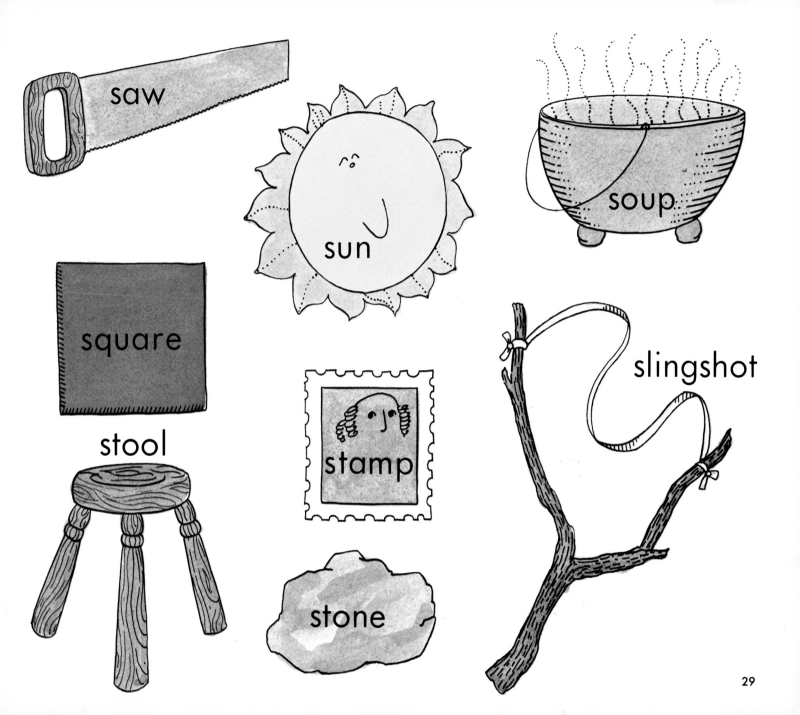

saw

sun

soup

square

slingshot

stool

stamp

stone

29

About the Author

Jane Belk Moncure, author of many books and stories for young children, is a graduate of Virginia Commonwealth University and Columbia University. She has taught nursery, kindergarten and primary children in Europe and America. Mrs. Moncure has taught early childhood education while serving on the faculties of Virginia Commonwealth University and the University of Richmond. She was the first president of the Virginia Association for Early Childhood Education and has been recognized widely for her services to young children. She is married to Dr. James A. Moncure, Vice President of Elon College, and currently teaches in Burlington, North Carolina.